新月集
The Crescent Moon

泰戈尔 - 著
Rabindranath Tagore works

伍晴文 - 译
Wu qingwen Translator

文汇出版社

图书在版编目（CIP）数据

新月集/（印）泰戈尔著；伍晴文译. -- 上海：文汇出版社，2016.5
ISBN 978-7-5496-1701-2

Ⅰ.①新… Ⅱ.①泰…②伍… Ⅲ.①诗集—印度—现代 Ⅳ.①I351.25

中国版本图书馆CIP数据核字（2016）第027707号

新月集

出 版 人 / 桂国强
作　　者 / 泰戈尔
责任编辑 / 戴　铮
封面装帧 / 粉粉猫
出版发行 / 文汇出版社
　　　　　 上海市威海路755号
　　　　　 （邮政编码200041）
经　　销 / 全国新华书店
印刷装订 / 三河市金泰源印务有限公司
版　　次 / 2016年5月第1版
印　　次 / 2016年5月第1次印刷
开　　本 / 889×1194　1/32
字　　数 / 92千字
印　　张 / 5.5

ISBN 978-7-5496-1701-2
定　价：29.00元

目录

01. 家 THE HOME 002

02. 海边 ON THE SEASHORE 006

03. 来源 THE SOURCE 010

04. 孩童之道 BABY'S WAY 014

05. 不受注意的盛典 THE UNHEEDED PAGEANT 018

06. 窃眠者 SLEEP-STEALER 024

07. 开始 THE BEGINNING 030

08. 孩子的世界 BABY'S WORLD 034

09. 时机与原因 WHEN AND WHY 038

10. 责备 DEFAMATION 042

046　11. 审判 THE JUDGE
048　12. 玩具 PLAYTHINGS
052　13. 天文学家 THE ASTRONOMER
056　14. 云与浪 CLOUDS AND WAVES
060　15. 金色花 THE CHAMPA FLOWER
066　16. 童话世界 FAIRYLAND
072　17. 流放之地 THE LAND OF THE EXILE
078　18. 雨天 THE RAINY DAY
082　19. 纸船 PAPER BOATS
086　20. 水手 THE SAILOR

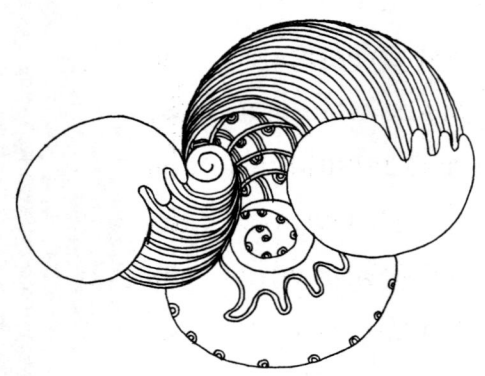

21. 对岸 THE FURTHER BANK　　090

22. 花的学校 THE FLOWER-SCHOOL　　094

23. 商人 THE MERCHANT　　098

24. 同情 SYMPATHY　　102

25. 职业 VOCATION　　106

26. 长者 SUPERIOR　　110

27. 小大人 THE LITTLE BIG MAN　　114

28. 十二点钟 TWELVE O'CLOCK　　120

29. 作者 AUTHORSHIP　　122

30. 坏邮差 THE WICKED POSTMAN　　126

130	31. 英雄	THE HERO
138	32. 告别	THE END
142	33. 呼唤	THE RECALL
146	34. 最初的茉莉	THE FIRST JASMINES
150	35. 榕树	THE BANYAN TREE
154	36. 祝福	BENEDICTION
156	37. 礼物	THE GIFT
158	38. 我的歌	MY SONG
162	39. 孩子天使	THE CHILD-ANGEL
166	40. 最后的买卖	THE LAST BARGAIN

01. 家

我独自漫步在穿过田野的小径上,夕阳像个守财奴,正藏起它最后一块金子。

白昼逐渐没入更深沉的黑暗中,而那已收割的寂地,静静躺在那儿。

顷刻间,有个男孩的高亢歌声响入云霄。他穿过看不见的黑幕,让歌声音韵回荡在夜晚的寂静中。

他村里的家就坐落在这块荒地底端,甘蔗园后边,隐藏在芭蕉、瘦长的槟榔树、椰子树和深绿色波罗蜜果树影里。

THE HOME

I paced alone on the road across the field while the sunset was hiding its last gold like a miser.

The daylight sank deeper and deeper into the darkness, and the widowed land, whose harvest had been reaped, lay silent.

Suddenly a boy's shrill voice rose into the sky. He traversed the dark unseen, leaving the track of his song across the hush of the evening.

His village home lay there at the end of the waste land, beyond the sugar-cane field, hidden among the shadows of the banana and the slender areca palm, the cocoa-nut and the dark green jack-fruit trees.

我在星空下的寂路上伫立了一会儿，看着暗沉的大地于我面前展开，用她的双臂揽抱无数个家庭，那里有摇篮和床，有母亲的心和夜灯，还有满心欢喜的年轻生命，浑然不知这欢乐对世界的价值。

I stopped for a moment in my lonely way under the starlight, and saw spread before me the darkened earth surrounding with her arms countless homes furnished with cradles and beds, mothers' hearts and evening lamps, and young lives glad with a gladness that knows nothing of its value for the world.

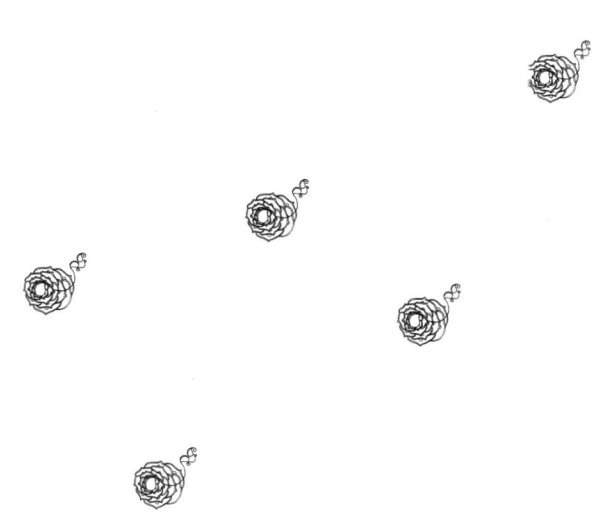

02. 海边

孩子们在无垠世界的海边相聚。

辽阔无边的穹苍凝止于头顶,奔流不息的海水喧嚷不休。孩子们在无垠世界的海边相聚,叫着、舞着。

他们拿沙造房子、拿空贝壳玩耍。他们拿落叶编织成船,笑着将之放入大海。孩子们在这世界的海边嬉游着。

他们不知如何游泳,也不知如何撒网。采珠人潜入海里采珠,商人驾着他们的船航行,而孩子们只是捡拾起小石头,又将之抛出。他们不去追寻宝藏,也不知如何撒网。

ON THE SEASHORE

On the seashore of endless worlds children meet.

The infinite sky is motionless overhead and the restless water is boisterous. On the seashore of endless worlds the children meet with shouts and dances.

They build their houses with sand, and they play with empty shells. With withered leaves they weave their boats and smilingly float them on the vast deep. Children have their play on the seashore of worlds.

They know not how to swim, they know not how to cast nets. Pearl-fishers dive for pearls, merchants sail in their ships, while children gather pebbles and scatter them again. They seek not for hidden treasures, they know not how to cast nets.

大海欢笑着卷起浪花,海滩的微笑闪耀着淡淡光芒。汹涌险恶的海浪对孩子们吟唱着无意义的歌曲,就像母亲轻推着她孩子的摇篮那样。大海陪孩子们玩耍,海滩的微笑闪耀着淡淡光芒。

孩子们在无垠世界的海边相聚。狂风暴雨扫过无痕的天空,船只沉碎在无痕的大海,死亡将近,而孩子们还在玩耍。孩子们在无垠世界的海边,欢乐地齐聚一处。

The sea surges up with laughter, and pale gleams the smile of the sea-beach. Death-dealing waves sing meaningless ballads to the children, even like a mother while rocking her baby's cradle. The sea plays with children, and pale gleams the smile of the sea-beach.

On the seashore of endless worlds children meet. Tempest roams in the pathless sky, ships are wrecked in the trackless water, death is abroad and children play. On the seashore of endless worlds is the great meeting of children.

03. 来源

掠过孩子双眸的睡眠——有谁知道它来自何方?是的,据传它栖息于森林阴影中有萤火虫微光照耀着的精灵村里,那里挂着两片迷人的羞怯花蕾。

它从那里前来亲吻孩子的双眸。

孩子睡着时,浮现在他双唇的那抹微笑——有谁知道它来自何方?

是的,据传新月那道新生的微光,触及将逝的秋云边缘,那抹微笑便是诞生于这沐浴露珠的晨梦里——孩子睡着时,浮现在他双唇的那抹微笑。

THE SOURCE

The sleep that flits on baby's eyes—does anybody know from where it comes? Yes, there is a rumour that it has its dwelling where, in the fairy village among shadows of the forest dimly lit with glow-worms, there hang two shy buds of enchantment.

From there it comes to kiss baby's eyes.

The smile that flickers on baby's lips when he sleeps—does anybody know where it was born?

Yes, there is a rumour that a young pale beam of a crescent moon touched the edge of a vanishing autumn cloud, and there the smile was first born in the dream of a dew-washed morning—the smile that flickers on baby's lips when he sleeps.

孩子四肢所绽放的那股芬芳又柔嫩的清新气息——有谁知道它藏在哪里藏了这么久?是的,当母亲还是少女时,它已潜伏在她心里,在爱的温柔与沉静的神秘里——孩子四肢所绽放的那股芬芳又柔嫩的清新气息。

The sweet, soft freshness that blooms on baby's limbs — does anybody know where it was hidden so long? Yes, when the mother was a young girl it lay pervading her heart in tender and silent mystery of love—the sweet, soft freshness that has bloomed on baby's limbs.

04. 孩童之道

只要孩子愿意,此刻便可飞上天堂。
他之所以不离开我们,并非毫无理由。
他喜欢将头倚靠在母亲怀中,半刻也不能看不见她。

孩子知道各种智慧之语,即使这世上极少人知晓其义。
他之所以从不想说话,并非毫无理由。
他想做的某一件事,便是学习从母亲唇间吐出的话语。
这也是他看起来如此天真的原因。

孩子坐拥成堆的金银珠宝,却像个乞儿似的来到这世界。
他之所以透过如此伪装来到这世界,并非毫无理由。

BABY'S WAY

If baby only wanted to, he could fly up to heaven this moment.

It is not for nothing that he does not leave us.

He loves to rest his head on mother's bosom, and cannot ever bear to lose sight of her.

Baby knows all manner of wise words, though few on earth can understand their meaning.

It is not for nothing that he never wants to speak.

The one thing he wants is to learn mother's words from mother's lips. That is why he looks so innocent.

Baby had a heap of gold and pearls, yet he came like a beggar on to this earth.

It is not for nothing he came in such a disguise.

这可爱的小乞儿，裸着身体装出一副全然无助的模样，这么一来他便可以向母亲乞求爱的财富。孩子在纤细的新月国度里，自由自在、毫无拘束。

他之所以放弃自由，并非毫无理由。

他知道母亲心窝有个小小的角落，藏着无穷无尽的欢乐，被母亲爱的臂弯紧紧拥住，可远比自由还要甜美。

孩子从不知如何哭泣。他住在极乐境邑里。

他之所以选择流泪，并非毫无理由。

虽然他可爱脸上的微笑，让母亲的心紧紧思系着他，但他因为小麻烦所发出的小小哭声，却织成怜悯与关爱的双重疼惜。

This dear little naked mendicant pretends to be utterly helpless, so that he may beg for mother's wealth of love.

Baby was so free from every tie in the land of the tiny crescent moon.

It was not for nothing he gave up his freedom.

He knows that there is room for endless joy in mother's little corner of a heart, and it is sweeter far than liberty to be caught and pressed in her dear arms.

Baby never knew how to cry. He dwelt in the land of perfect bliss.

It is not for nothing he has chosen to shed tears.

Though with the smile of his dear face he draws mother's yearning heart to him, yet his little cries over tiny troubles weave the double bond of pity and love.

05. 不受注意的盛典

啊,谁把那身小衣裳染上颜色的,我的孩子,谁在你那惹人喜爱的四肢套上那件小红衫?

你一早便跑到庭院玩耍,跑的时候跌跌又撞撞。

但究竟是谁把那身小衣裳染上颜色的,我的孩子?

什么事逗你笑了,我生命的小花蕾?

母亲站在门边对你露出微笑。

她拍着手,腕上的镯子叮当作响,而你拿着竹竿手舞足蹈,活像个小牧童。

但究竟是什么事逗你笑了,我生命的小花蕾?

THE UNHEEDED PAGEANT

Ah, who was it coloured that little frock, my child, and covered your sweet limbs with that little red tunic?

You have come out in the morning to play in the courtyard, tottering and tumbling as you run.

But who was it coloured that little frock, my child?

What is it makes you laugh, my little life-bud?

Mother smiles at you standing on the threshold.

She claps her hands and her bracelets jingle, and you dance whth your bamboo stick in your hand like a tiny little shepherd.

But what is it makes you laugh, my little life-bud?

喔，小乞儿，你双手搂着妈妈的脖子想要乞求些什么？

喔，贪婪的心儿，要我把整个世界从天上摘下来，像摘果实般放在你小小的红嫩掌心上吗？

喔，小乞儿，你想要乞求些什么？

风欢欢喜喜地带走了你踝铃的叮当声。

太阳微笑地看着你梳洗。

当你在母亲的臂弯里睡着时，天空从上护望着你，早晨蹑手蹑脚来到你床前，亲吻着你的双眼。

风欢欢喜喜地带走了你踝铃的叮当声。

O beggar, what do you beg for, clinging to your mother's neck with both your hands?

O greedy heart, shall I pluck the world like a fruit from the sky to place it on your little rosy palm?

O beggar, what are you begging for?

The wind carries away in glee the tinkling of your anklet bells.

The sun smiles and watches your toilet.

The sky watches over you when you sleep in your mother's arms, and the morning comes tiptoe to your bed and kisses your eyes.

The wind carries away in glee the tinkling of your anklet bells.

梦中精灵正穿过微明的天空,朝你飞来呢。

世界之母在你母亲心中,保留了在你身旁的位置。

那个向群星演奏音乐的人,正拿着他的长笛站在你窗前。

梦中精灵正穿过微明的天空,朝你飞来呢。

The fairy mistress of dreams is coming towards you, flying through the twilight sky.

The world-mother keeps her seat by you in your mother's heart.

He who plays his music to the stars i s standing at your window with his flute.

And the fairy mistress of dreams is coming towards you, flying through the twilight sky.

06. 窃眠者

谁从孩子的双眸偷走了睡眠?我一定得知道。

母亲将水罐挟在腰间,到附近村庄汲水。

那是正午时分,孩子玩耍的时间已经过了,池塘里的鸭子寂静无声。

牧童躺在榕树的荫下睡着了。

白鹤沉静地站在芒果园旁的沼泽中。

就在此时,窃眠者过来从孩子的双眸偷走睡眠,飞走了。

当母亲回来时,发现孩子四肢着地在屋里爬着。

是谁从孩子的双眸偷走了睡眠?我一定得知道。我得找到她并绑住她。

SLEEP-STEALER

Who stole sleep from baby's eyes? I must know.

Clasping her pitcher to her waist, mother went to fetch water from the village near by.

It was noon. The children's playtime was over; the ducks in the pond were silent.

The shepherd boy lay asleep under the shadow of the banyan tree.

The crane stood grave and still in the swamp near the mango grove.

In the meanwhile the Sleep-stealer came and, snatching sleep from baby's eyes, flew away.

When mother came back she found baby travelling the room over on all fours.

Who stole sleep from our baby's eyes? I must know. I must find her and chain her up.

我得到黑洞那儿找找,洞里的水滴淌过圆卵石和沉石,汇聚成一泓小溪流。

我一定得到醉花丛那沉寂的荫影处找找,鸽子在它们栖息的角落咕咕叫着,精灵的脚环叮当响彻满天星斗的寂静夜空。

入夜后,我会到寂语喃喃的竹林窥看。萤火虫在那里挥霍它们的光芒,我会向我遇见的每一个生物问:"有谁能告诉我窃眠者住在哪里吗?"

谁从孩子的双眸偷走了睡眠?我一定得知道。

假如我能抓到她,肯定要好好教训她!

我要闯入她的老巢,看看她把所有偷来的睡眠都藏到哪儿去了。

我要将之全部夺回。

I must look into that dark cave, where, through boulders and scowling stones, trickles a tiny stream.

I must search in the drowsy shade of the bakula grove, where pigeons coo in their corner, and fairies' anklets tinkle in the stillness of starry nights.

In the evening I will peep into the whispering silence of the bamboo forest, where fireflies squander their light, and will ask every creature I meet, " Can anybody tell me where the Sleep-stealer lives? "

Who stole sleep from baby's eyes? I must know.

Shouldn't I give her a good lesson if I could only catch her!

I would raid her nest and see where she hoards all her stolen sleep.

I would plunder it all, and carry it home.

我会将她的两翼牢牢缚住,将她放在河岸边,让她在灯心草与睡莲间拿着一根芦苇乖乖玩钓鱼游戏。

当市场于晚间收市后,村里的孩子坐在母亲膝上时,夜鸟将来到她耳边嘲弄地呱叫道:"现在你想偷谁的睡眠呀?"

I would bind her two wings securely, set her on the bank of the river, and then let her play at fishing with a reed among the rushes and water-lilies.

When the marketing is over in the evening, and the village children sit in their mothers' laps, then the night birds will mockingly din her ears with:"Whose sleep will you steal now?"

07. 开始

"我是从哪里来的?您在哪里捡到我的呢?"孩子问妈妈。

她把孩子抱在胸前,又哭又笑地回答说:

"你曾像我的心愿般,藏在我心底,我亲爱的宝贝。

你曾藏在我孩童时玩的小土偶里;我每天早上用泥土捏出的神像,那个我当时捏好了又捏碎的就是你。

你跟我们家的神明一同被供奉着,在祭拜家神的同时,也祭拜了你。

你一直活在我所有的希望和爱中,活在我的生命和我母亲的生命里。

你已经在主导着我们家永垂不朽的神灵膝上,被抚育了世世代代。

THE BEGINNING

"Where have I come from, where did you pick me up?" the baby asked its mother.

She answered half crying, half laughing, and clasping the baby to her breast, —

"You were hidden in my heart as its desire, my darling.

You were in the dolls of my childhood's games; and when with clay I made the image of my god every morning, I made and unmade you then.

You were enshrined with our household deity, in his worship I worshipped you.

In all my hopes and my loves, in my life, in the life of my mother you have lived.

In the lap of the deathless Spirit who rules our home you have been nursed for ages.

当我还是少女,心如花瓣绽开时,你就像花香常伴左右。

你稚嫩的柔软在我青春的肢体上绽放开来,就像日出前,洒现在空中的光芒。

你是天堂里最受宠、与晨曦一同诞生的孪生兄弟,你随着世界的生命之流浮游而下,最后终于停在我心头。

当我凝视着你的脸时,那股神秘感震撼着我;原属于所有人的你,竟变成了我的。

我因害怕失去你,而将你紧紧抱在怀里。是什么魔法将世界的宝贝引领至我细弱的双臂里?"

When in girlhood my heart was opening its petals, you hovered as a fragrance about it.

Your tender softness bloomed in my youthful limbs, like a glow in the sky before the sunrise.

Heaven's first darling, twin-born with the morning light, you have floated down the stream of the world's life, and at last you have stranded on my heart.

As I gaze on your face, mystery overwhelms me; you who belong to all have become mine.

For fear of losing you I hold you tight to my breast. What magic has snared the world's treasure in these slender arms of mine? "

08. 孩子的世界

我愿自己能在孩子的内心世界占一个安静的角落。

我知道星辰会和他说话,天空也会俯身到他面前,用那傻傻的云朵和彩虹来逗弄他。

那些让人以为不会说话和看似永不会动弹的家伙,带着他们的故事、捧着摆满亮丽玩具的盘子,悄悄爬到他窗前。

BABY'S WORLD

I wish I could take a quiet corner in the heart of my baby's very own world.

I know it has stars that talk to him, and a sky that stoops down to his face to amuse him with its silly clouds and rainbows.

Those who make believe to be dumb, and look as if they never could move, come creeping to his window with their stories and with trays crowded with bright toys.

但愿我能行走于穿越孩子心中的道路上,毫无障碍;

在那里,使者徒然奔走于没有历史的君主王国间;

在那里,理智将她的律法当作风筝放飞,真理也让事实摆脱束缚,得获自由。

I wish I could travel by the road that crosses baby's mind, and out beyond all bounds;

Where messengers run errands for no cause between the kingdoms of kings of no history;

Where Reason makes kites of her laws and flies them, and Truth sets Fact free from its fetters.

09. 时机与原因

当我拿那些彩色玩具给你时，我的孩子，我这才了解云间、水上为什么会如此缤纷，为什么花朵会渲染上色彩——当我拿那些彩色玩具给你时，我的孩子。

当我唱歌让你欢舞时，我这才真正了解叶子上为什么会响出音律，为什么浪涛要将它们合唱的乐声传送到静静聆听的心上——当我唱歌让你欢舞时。

当我将那些糖果放到你贪心的手掌时，我这才了解花萼里为什么会有蜜液，果实里为什么会藏着甜汁——当我将那些糖果放到你贪心的手掌时。

WHEN AND WHY

When I bring you coloured toys, my child, I understand why there is such a play of colours on clouds, on water, and why flowers are painted in tints—when I give coloured toys to you, my child.

When I sing to make you dance, I truly know why there is music in leaves, and why waves send their chorus of voices to the heart of the listening earth—when I sing to make you dance.

When I bring sweet things to your greedy hands, I know why there is honey in the cup of the flower, and why fruits are secretly filled with sweet juice—when I bring sweet things to your greedy hands.

当我亲吻你的脸蛋逗你微笑时,我亲爱的宝贝,我这才真正明白晨光从天空带来什么样的欢乐,夏日微风为我的身躯带来什么样的欢愉——当我亲吻你逗你微笑时。

When I kiss your face to make you smile, my darling, I surely understand what pleasure streams from the sky in morning light, and what delight the summer breeze brings to my body—when I kiss you to make you smile.

10. 责备

你的眼中为何盈满眼泪,我的孩子?

总是平白无故责备你是多么可怕的事情呀!

你写字时手指及小脸沾上了墨水——他们是因为这样说你脏兮兮的吗?

喔,呸!

要是满月的脸上沾了墨水,他们也胆敢嫌它脏吗?

他们吹毛求疵地责备你,我的孩子。他们总是爱在鸡蛋里挑骨头。

你玩耍的时候扯破了衣裳——他们是因为这样说你邋遢的吗?

DEFAMATION

Why are those tears in your eyes, my child?

How horrid of them to be always scolding you for nothing!

You have stained your fingers and face with ink while writing—is that why they call you dirty?

O, fie!

Would they dare to call the full moon dirty because it has smudged its face with ink?

For every little trifle they blame you, my child. They are ready to find fault for nothing.

You tore your clothes while playing—is that why they call you untidy?

喔,呸!秋天早晨从它的碎云中露出微笑,那他们要怎么怪它呢?

别在意他们对你说的话,我的孩子。

他们列了一长串你的罪行。大家都知道你喜欢糖果——他们是因为这样说你贪心的吗?

喔,呸!我们是如此爱你,他们又要怎么数落我们这些人呢?

O, fie! What would they call an autumn morning that smiles through its ragged clouds?

Take no heed of what they say to you, my child

They make a long list of your misdeeds.

Everybody knows how you love sweet things—is that why they call you greedy?

O, fie! What then would they call us who love you?

11. 审判

你爱怎么说他就怎么说他吧,但是我清楚知道自己孩子的缺点。

我不是因为他好才爱他的,而是因为他是我的小小孩。

如果只是衡量他的优缺点,你怎会知道他有多可爱?

当我需要责罚他时,他已成为我生命的一部分。

当我让他流下眼泪时,我的心也跟着他流泪。

只有我自己有权责罚他,因为唯有深爱他的人才能惩罚他。

THE JUDGE

Say of him what you please, but I know my child's failings.

I do not love him because he is good, but because he is my little child.

How should you know how dear he can be when you try to weigh his merits against his faults?

When I must punish him he becomes all the more a part of my being.

When I cause his tears to come my heart weeps with him.

I alone have a right to blame and punish, for he only may chastise who loves.

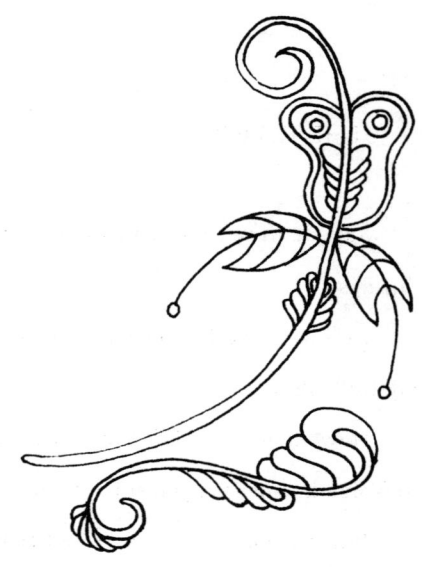

12. 玩具

孩子,你一整个早上坐在泥土上玩着断枝,该有多快乐呀。

我微笑地看着你玩那小小的断枝儿。

我正忙着算账,一个小时又一个小时加算着数字。

或许你会看着我想道:"为什么要玩这无聊的游戏,破坏自己美好的早晨!"

孩子,我已经忘记专心玩树枝与泥巴的方法了。

我追求着昂贵的玩具,收集金块与银块。

PLAYTHINGS

Child, how happy you are sitting in the dust, playing with a broken twig all the morning.

I smile at your play with that little bit of a broken twig.

I am busy with my accounts, adding up figures by the hour.

Perhaps you glance at me and think,"What a stupid game to spoil your morning with! "

Child, I have forgotten the art of being absorbed in sticks and mud-pies.

I seek out costly playthings, and gather lumps of gold and silver.

无论找到什么,你总能够创造出快乐无比的游戏,而我啊,却总是将自己的时间与力气花费在我永远也得不到的事物上。

我在这艘摇摇欲坠的独木舟上,挣扎地穿越欲望之海,竟忘了自己也在其中游戏哩。

With whatever you find you create your glad games, I spend both my time and my strength over things I never can obtain.

In my frail canoe I struggle to cross the sea of desire, and forget that I too am playing a game.

13. 天文学家

我只不过说:"当夜晚满月缠挂在伽昙波树的枝头时,难道没有人能将它抓下吗?"

哥哥却笑着对我说:"小宝贝,你是我见过最傻的孩子了。月亮离我们那么远,有谁能抓得到它呢?"

我说:"哥哥你真傻!当妈妈望向窗外,往下笑着看我们玩时,你会说她离我们很远吗?"

哥哥还是说:"你真是个傻孩子!但是,小宝贝,你到哪儿去找一张大得可以捕住月亮的网呢?"

THE ASTRONOMER

I only said, "When in the evening the round full moon gets entangled among the branches of that Kadam tree, couldn't somebody catch it?"

But dada [elder brother] laughed at me and said, "Baby, you are the silliest child I have ever known. The moon is ever so far from us, how could anybody catch it?"

I said, "Dada, how foolish you are! When mother looks out of her window and smiles down at us playing, would you call her far away?"

Still dada said, "You are a stupid child! But, baby, where could you find a net big enough to catch the moon with?"

我说:"双手就能够抓住月亮啦。"

可是哥哥笑着说道:"你是我见过最傻的孩子了。等月亮靠近时,你就会晓得月亮有多大了。"

我说:"哥哥,他们在学校可真是教了你一些没用的东西!当妈妈低下脸来亲吻我们时,她的脸看起来也很大吗?"

但哥哥还是说:"你真是个傻孩子。"

I said,"Surely you could catch it with your hands."

But dada laughed and said,"You are the silliest child I have known. If it came nearer, you would see how big the moon is."

I said,"Dada, what nonsense they teach at your school! When mother bends her face down to kiss us does her face look very big?"

But still dada says,"You are a stupid child."

14. 云与浪

母亲，住在云端上的那些人对我喊道：

"我们从醒来那一刻玩到白昼终了。我们跟金黄色的曙光玩耍、跟银白色的月亮嬉戏。"

我问道："可是，我怎提么才能到你们那里去呢？"

他们回答："到地球的边缘，将双手举向天，你就会被拉到云端上了。"

"我妈妈在家等着我呢，"我说，"我怎能离开她来到你们身边呀？"

他们接着便笑了笑，飘离开了。

但我知道一个比这更好玩的游戏，母亲。

我当云，您当月亮。

CLOUDS AND WAVES

Mother, the folk who live up in the clouds call out to me—

"We play from the time we wake till the day ends. We play with the golden dawn, we play with the silver moon. "

I ask,"But, how am I to get up to you? "

They answer,"Come to the edge of the earth, lift up your hands to the sky, and you will be taken up into the clouds. "

"My mother is waiting for me at home,"I say."How can I leave her and come? "

Then they smile and float away.

But I know a nicer game than that, mother.

I shall be the cloud and you the moon.

我用双手遮住您,我们的屋顶就是湛蓝的天空。

住在波浪上的那些人对我喊道:

"我们从早唱到晚,一直走着路,不知道自己经过了些什么地方。"

我问道:"可是,我要怎么才能到你们那里去呢?"

他们跟我说:"到海岸边,紧闭着双眼站在那里,波浪就会把你拉上来了。"

我说:"我的母亲总希望我晚上好好待在家里——我怎能离开她,跟你们走呢?"

他们接着便笑了笑,舞着离开了。

但我知道一个比这更好玩的游戏。

我当海浪,您当那陌生的海岸。

我会一次又一次滚到岸边,笑着撞您的膝。

世上没有人知道我们在哪里。

I shall cover you with both my hands, and our house-top will be the blue sky.

✡

The folk who live in the waves call out to me—

"We sing from morning till night; on and on we travel and know not where we pass. "

I ask,"But, how am I to join you? "

They tell me,"Come to the edge of the shore and stand with your eyes tight shut, and you will be carried out upon the waves. "

I say,"My mother always wants me at home in the evening—how can I leave her and go? "

Then they smile, dance and pass by.

But I know a better game than that.

I will be the waves and you will be a strange shore.

I shall roll on and on and on, and break upon your lap with laughter.

And no one in the world will know where we both are.

15. 金色花

假设我纯为了好玩而变成一朵金色花①,长在那高高的枝头上,笑着随风摇曳,在新生的叶子上舞动着,您还会认得我吗,妈妈?

您可能会喊道:"宝贝呀,你在哪里?"而我会一声不响地躲在那里暗自偷笑。

我会悄悄打开花瓣,看着您工作。

当您沐浴完,湿发还披落在双肩时,您走过金色花下的林荫,来到祷告的小庭院,您会闻到花朵香气,却不知道那是我散发出来的。

THE CHAMPA FLOWER

Supposing I became a champa flower, just for fun, and grew on a branch high up that tree, and shook in the wind with laughter and danced upon the newly budded leaves, would you know me, mother?

You would call,"Baby, where are you? "and I should laugh to myself and keep quite quiet.

I should slyly open my petals and watch you at your work.

When after your bath, with wet hair spread on your shoulders, you walked through the shadow of the champa tree to the little court where you say your prayers, you would notice the scent of the flower, but not know that it came from me.

午饭过后,当您坐在窗前读着《罗摩衍那》[2]时,树影落在您的头发与膝上,我会在您的书页中投下我小小的影子,就刚好落在您正读到的地方。

但是您会猜得到这是您孩子的小小身影吗?

When after the midday meal you sat at the window reading Ramayana , and the tree's shadow fell over your hair and your lap, I should fling my wee little shadow on to the page of your book, just where you were reading.

But would you guess that it was the tiny shadow of your little child?

到了晚上,当您手拿着灯到牛棚时,我会突然又跳回人间,再度变成了您的宝贝,求您跟我讲故事。

"你跑到哪儿去啦,你这淘气的孩子?"

"我不告诉您,妈妈。"那将会是您和我的对话。

---

① 此处"金色花"的原文为 Champa Flower,为印度圣树所产之花,木兰科含笑属,一般称"黄玉兰",云南一带又可叫作"缅桂花"。
② 《罗摩衍那》(Ramayana)是印度两大史诗之一,另一部为《摩诃婆罗多》(Mahabharata)。

When in the evening you went to the cow-shed with the lighted lamp in your hand, I should suddenly drop on to the earth again and be your own baby once more, and beg you to tell me a story.

"Where have you been, you naughty child?"

"I won't tell you, mother." That's what you and I would say then.

16. 童话世界

如果让人们知道了我的国王宫殿在哪里,宫殿便会消失无踪。

墙壁是白银打造的,屋顶则是灿烂的黄金。

皇后住在有七进院落的宫殿里,穿戴着整整与七个王国等值的珠宝。

但让我告诉您,母亲,让我偷偷地告诉您我的国王宫殿在哪里。

FAIRYLAND

If people came to know where my king's palace is, it would vanish into the air.

The walls are of white silver and the roof of shining gold.

The queen lives in a palace with seven courtyards, and she wears a jewel that cost all the wealth of seven kingdoms.

But let me tell you, mother, in a whisper, where my king's palace is.

它就在我们阳台上放着圣罗勒盆栽的那个角落。

公主在七海之外那处遥不可及的岸边沉睡着。

这世界上除了我,再没有人能找得到她。

她腕上戴着手镯,耳朵挂着珍珠,秀发长曳在地。

我拿着魔杖向她一点,她便会醒来;而当她微笑时,珠宝就会从她双唇落下。

但是母亲,让我在您耳边偷偷告诉您,她就在我们阳台上放着圣罗勒盆栽的那个角落。

It is at the corner of our terrace where the pot of the tulsi plant stands.

The princess lies sleeping on the far-away shore of the seven impassable seas.

There is none in the world who can find her but myself.

She has bracelets on her arms and pearl drops in her ears; her hair sweeps down upon the floor.

She will wake when I touch her with my magic wand, and jewels will fall from her lips when she smiles.

But let me whisper in your ear, mother; she is there in the corner of our terrace where the pot of the tulsi plant stands.

到了您该去河边沐浴的时刻,走上屋顶阳台吧。

我就坐在各面墙影交会的角落。

我只准小猫跟随我一起来,因为她知道故事里的理发匠住在哪儿。

但是母亲,让我在您耳边偷偷告诉您,故事里的理发匠住在哪儿吧!

就在我们阳台上放着圣罗勒盆栽的那个角落哦。

When it is time for you to go to the river for your bath, step up to that terrace on the roof.

I sit in the corner where the shadows of the walls meet together.

Only puss is allowed to come with me, for she knows where the barber in the story lives.

But let me whisper, mother, in your ear where the barber in the story lives.

It is at the corner of the terrace where the pot of the tulsi plant stands.

17. 流放之地

妈妈,天色变暗了,
我不知道现在几点钟。
我的游戏有点无聊了,所以我来找您。今天是周六,我们的休假日。
放下您手边的工作吧,妈妈,坐到窗边来,告诉我童话故事里的特潘塔沙漠在哪里。

雨的影子遮盖了整个白天。
可怕的闪电用它的爪子抓住天空。
当乌云轰隆隆地打起雷时,我喜欢怀着恐惧依偎在您身边。

THE LAND OF THE EXILE

Mother, the light has grown grey in the sky. I do not know what the time is.

There is no fun in my play, so I have come to you. It is Saturday, our holiday.

Leave off your work, mother; sit here by the window and tell me where the desert of Tepantar in the fairy tale is?

The shadow of the rains has covered the day from end to end.

The fierce lightning is scratching the sky with its nails.

When the clouds rumble and it thunders, I love to be afraid in my heart and cling to you.

当大雨噼里啪啦在竹叶上打了好几个小时,窗户也被狂风震得格格作响时,我喜欢单独和您坐在房里,妈妈,听您讲童话中特潘塔沙漠里发生的故事。

那沙漠到底在哪里呢,妈妈?在哪座海洋的岸边,哪座山的脚下,还是哪位国王的王国里?

那里没有篱笆围界田园,也没有路让村民于日落时分穿过田野回村庄,或者让在林子里拾干材的妇女运载到市场去。沙地上只有几块黄草地及一棵树,一对聪明的老鸟在树上头筑了个巢,特潘塔沙漠就在那里。

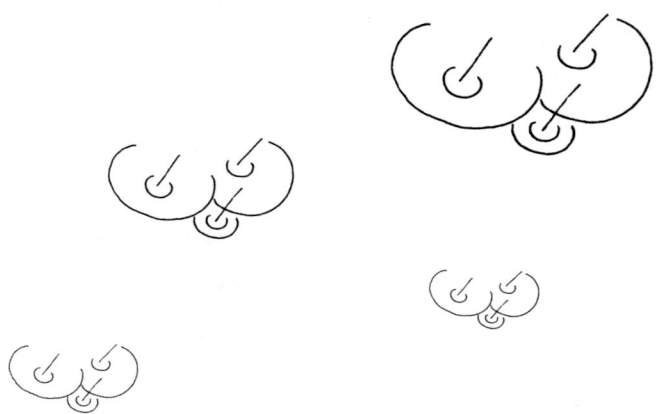

When the heavy rain patters for hours on the bamboo leaves, and our windows shake and rattle at the gusts of wind, I like to sit alone in the room, mother, with you, and hear you talk about the desert of Tepantar in the fairy tale.

Where is it, mother, on the shore of what sea, at the foot of what hills, in the kingdom of what king?

There are no hedges there to mark the fields, no footpath across it by which the villagers reach their village in the evening, or the woman who gathers dry sticks in the forest can bring her load to the market. With patches of yellow grass in the sand and only one tree where the pair of wise old birds have their nest, lies the desert of Tepantar.

我可以想象在这样乌云密布的天气，国王的那个小儿子如何独自骑着那匹灰马穿过沙漠，横越不知名的海域，寻找被囚禁在巨人宫里的公主。

雨雾于遥远天际降下，闪电像一阵突如其来的痛楚发作，当他骑过童话故事里的特潘塔沙漠时，可否想起自己被国王抛弃的不幸母亲，正在清扫着牛棚、拭着眼泪？

看呀，妈妈，白昼还未结束，天色就已经快黑了，村庄的路上没有什么人。

牧羊童早早从牧场回家了，人们也已从田里返回，坐在他们小屋屋檐下的草席上，望着阴沉的乌云。

妈妈，我把所有书都丢在书架上——别要我现在去做功课。

等我长大，大得像爸爸时，我自然便能学会所有该学的了。

但是，妈妈，就今天，赶紧告诉我童话故事里的特潘塔沙漠在哪里吧？

I can imagine how, on just such a cloudy day, the young son of the king is riding alone on a grey horse through the desert, in search of the princess who lies imprisoned in the giant's palace across that unknown water.

When the haze of the rain comes down in the distant sky, and lightning starts up like a sudden fit of pain, does he remember his unhappy mother, abandoned by the king, sweeping the cow-stall and wiping her eyes, while he rides through the desert of Tepantar in the fairy tale?

See, mother, it is almost dark before the day is over, and there are no travellers yonder on the village road.

The shepherd boy has gone home early from the pasture, and men have left their fields to sit on mats under the eaves of their huts, watching the scowling clouds.

Mother, I have left all my books on the shelf—do not ask me to do my lessons now.

When I grow up and am big like my father, I shall learn all that must be learnt.

But just for to-day, tell me, mother, where the desert of Tepantar in the fairy tale is?

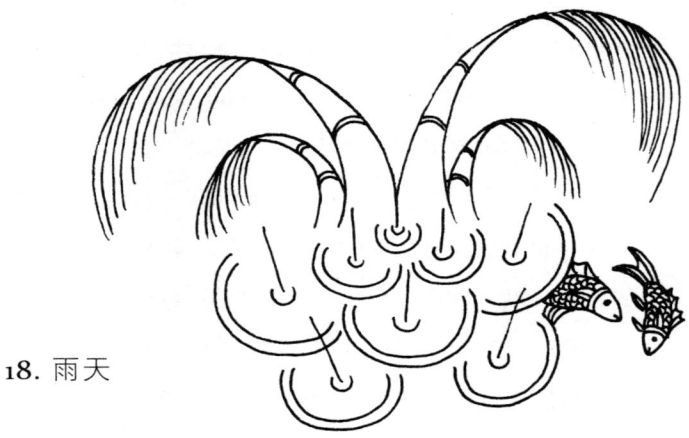

18. 雨天

黑压压的乌云快速聚集在森林那黑色边缘。

喔,孩子,别跑出去!

湖边那一排棕榈树正把头撞向那一片黑压压的天空;双翅脏乱的乌鸦静静地停在罗望树枝上,渐深的黑沉袭往河的东岸。

我们绑在篱笆旁的牛,大声地哞叫着。

喔,孩子,在这里等着,等我把牛牵进牛棚。

人们已经聚集在淹满水的田间,准备抓从涨溢池塘里跑出来的鱼儿。雨水汇成涓涓水流,流过狭窄街巷,就像一个笑闹着的孩子,从母亲身边跑开,故意惹她生气。

THE RAINY DAY

Sullen clouds are gathering fast over the black fringe of the forest.

O child, do not go out!

The palm trees in a row by the lake are smiting their heads against the dismal sky; the crows with their draggled wings are silent on the tamarind branches, and the eastern bank cf the river is haunted by a deepening gloom.

Our cow is lowing loud, tied at the fence.

O child, wait here till I bring her into the stall.

Men have crowded into the flooded field to catch the fishes as they escape from the overflowing ponds; the rain water is running in rills through the narrow lanes like a laughing boy who has run away from his mother to tease her.

听呀,有人从渡口浅滩呼喊着船夫哩。

喔,孩子,日光渐暗,渡口的摆渡也休止了。

天空好像在疯狂倾泻的大雨中奔跑着,河水又大又急,妇女们早就从恒河装满水匆匆回家了。

晚上要用的灯,记得先准备好。

喔,孩子,别跑出去!

往市场的路已毫无人烟,往河畔的路很滑。风在竹枝间咆哮、挣扎着,就像一只被困在网子里的野兽。

Listen, someone is shouting for the boatman at the ford.

O child, the daylight is dim, and the crossing at the ferry is closed.

The sky seems to ride fast upon the madly-rushing rain; the water in the river is loud and impatient; women have hastened home early from the Ganges with their filled pitchers.

The evening lamps must be made ready.

O child, do not go out!

The road to the market is desolate, the lane to the river is slippery. The wind is roaring and struggling among the bamboo branches like a wild beast tangled in a net.

19. 纸船

我日复一日将我的纸船一只只放入潺潺溪水中。

以大大的黑字书写上我的名字及我所住村庄之名。

希望在陌生土地上的某个人能发现这些船,还知道我是谁。

我从我们园子里摘了束秀利花放在我的小船上,希望这批拂晓绽放的花朵,到了夜里能被安全地带上岸。

PAPER BOATS

Day by day I float my paper boats one by one down the running stream.

In big black letters I write my name on them and the name of the village where I live.

I hope that someone in some strange land will find them and know who I am.

I load my little boats with shiuli flowers from our garden, and hope that these blooms of the dawn will be carried safely to land in the night.

我将我的纸船放到河里,抬头仰望天空,看着小小云朵扬起它们张鼓的白帆。

我不知道自个儿在天上有什么玩伴,将这些船放下来和我的船比赛!

入夜之后,我将脸埋进臂弯里,梦见我的纸船在午夜星空下漂流向前。

睡梦仙子坐在这一艘艘船上,带着装满梦的篮子。

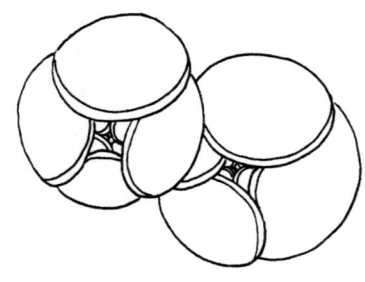

I launch my paper boats and look up into the sky and see the little clouds setting their white bulging sails.

I know not what playmate of mine in the sky sends them down the air to race with my boats!

When night comes I bury my face in my arms and dream that my paper boats float on and on under the midnight stars.

The fairies of sleep are sailing in them, and the lading is their baskets full of dreams.

20. 水手

船夫马杜的船停放在拉古尼码头。

船上装满一无用处的黄麻,已闲置在那儿好长一段时间了。

要是他愿意把船借给我,我会为它装上一百支船桨,扬起五面六面或七面船帆。

我绝不会将这艘船开进愚蠢的市集。

我要航向童话世界里的七大洋与十三条江河。

然而,妈妈,您别躲在角落为我哭泣。

我不会像罗摩犍陀罗①跑到森林里,十四年后才回来。

THE SAILOR

The boat of the boatman Madhu is moored at the wharf of Rajgunj.

It is uselessly laden with jute, and has been lying there idle for ever so long.

If he would only lend me his boat, I should man her with a hundred oars, and hoist sails, five or six or seven.

I should never steer her to stupid markets.

I should sail the seven seas and the thirteen rivers of fairyland.

But, mother, you won't weep for me in a corner.

I am not going into the forest like Ramachandra to come back only after fourteen years.

我将变成故事中的王子,船上载满我喜欢的东西。

我还会带上我的朋友阿苏,一起快快乐乐地航行过童话故事里的七大洋与十三条江河。

我们会在破晓晨曦中扬帆出发。

当您午间在池中沐浴时,我们应该已到了一个陌生的国度。

我们会经过特普尼滩,将特潘塔沙漠抛在我们身后。

当天色渐暗,我们归来之时,我会告诉您许多我们的所见所闻。

我将航行过童话故事里的七大洋与十三条江河。

---

① 即《罗摩衍那》史诗的主角罗摩,亦是主神毗湿奴的众多化身之一。故事中,罗摩和妻子退居森林十四年,与魔王相抗、夺回妻子后才登上王位。

I shall become the prince of the story, and fill my boat with whatever I like.

I shall take my friend Ashu with me. We shall sail merrily across the seven seas and the thirteen rivers of fairyland.

We shall set sail in the early morning light.

When at noontide you are bathing at the pond, we shall be in the land of a strange king.

We shall pass the ford of Tirpurni, and leave behind us the desert of Tepantar.

When we come back it will be getting dark, and I shall tell you of all that we have seen.

I shall cross the seven seas and the thirteen rivers of fairyland.

21. 对岸

我渴望到河对岸去。
那里有一整排船绑在竹竿上；
人们早上划着船过河，肩扛着锄头到远处田地里耕作；
那里的牧人赶着哞哞叫的牛涉水游到对岸的牧场；
傍晚时他们全都回家了，只留下豺狼在长满野草的岛上嚎叫着。
母亲，如果您不介意，我长大以后想成为这渡口的船夫。

人们说高岸后面藏着些奇怪的池塘。
一群群的野鸭总会在雨后飞到那里去，池边长满了芦苇，水鸟会在那儿下蛋；

THE FURTHER BANK

I long to go over there to the further bank of the river,

Where those boats are tied to the bamboo poles in a line;

Where men cross over in their boats in the morning with ploughs on their shoulders to till their far-away fields;

Where the cowherds make their lowing cattle swim across to the riverside pasture;

Whence they all come back home in the evening, leaving the jackals to howl in the island overgrown with weeds.

Mother, if you don't mind, I should like to become the boatman of the ferry when I am grown up.

They say there are strange pools hidden behind that high bank.

Where flocks of wild ducks come when the rains are over, and thick reeds grow round the margins where waterbirds lay their eggs;

竹鸡会摇摆着尾巴,将它们小小的足印留在干净的软泥上;

入夜后,长草顶着白花,邀请月光荡游在它们的草波间。

母亲,如果您不介意,我长大以后想成为这渡口的船夫。

我将往返于两岸,村里所有在河中沐浴的男孩与女孩,都惊奇地看着我。

当太阳爬上了半空,清晨变为中午时,我会跑向您喊着:"妈妈,我饿了!"

待一天结束,影子蜷伏在树下时,我会踏着暮色回家。

我铁定不会像爸爸那样离开您到城里工作。

母亲,如果您不介意,我长大以后想成为这渡口的船夫。

Where snipes with their dancing tails stamp their tiny footprints upon the clean soft mud;

Where in the evening the tall grasses crested with white flowers invite the moonbeam to float upon their waves.

Mother, if you don't mind, I should like to become the boatman of the ferryboat when I am grown up.

I shall cross and cross back from bank to bank, and all the boys and girls of the village will wonder at me while they are bathing.

When the sun climbs the mid sky and morning wears on to noon, I shall come running to you, saying,"Mother, I am hungry! "

When the day is done and the shadows cower under the trees, I shall come back in the dusk.

I shall never go away from you into the town to work like father.

Mother, if you don't mind, I should like to become the boatman of the ferryboat when I am grown up.

22. 花的学校

当雷云在空中轰轰作响，落下六月阵雨时，湿润的东风吹过荒野，在竹林间吹奏它的风笛。

一堆花朵突然不知从哪儿冒了出来，在绿草上狂欢跳舞着。

THE FLOWER-SCHOOL

When storm clouds rumble in the sky and June showers come down, The moist east wind comes marching over the heath to blow its bagpipes among the bamboos.

Then crowds of flowers come out of a sudden, from nobody knows where, and dance upon the grass in wild glee.

妈妈，我真的认为那些花朵是在地底的学校上学。

它们关上门做功课，如果它们想在放学前跑出来玩，老师就会要它们在墙角罚站。

一下雨，它们便放假了。

林里的枝叶交错在一起，树叶在狂风中簌簌作响，雷云拍打着巨大的手，花孩子们即穿上粉红色、黄色和白色的衣服冲了出来。

您知道么，母亲，它们的家在天空上，在星星住的地方。

您没看到它们如何急着到那里去吗？您难道不知道它们为何如此匆忙吗？

我当然猜得出来它们是对谁张开手臂的：它们其实就跟我一样，也有自己的妈妈。

Mother, I really think the flowers go to school underground.

They do their lessons with doors shut, and if they want to come out to play before it is time, their master makes them stand in a corner.

When the rains come they have their holidays.

Branches clash together in the forest, and the leaves rustle in the wild wind, the thunder-clouds clap their giant hands and the flower children rush out in dresses of pink and yellow and white.

Do you know, mother, their home is in the sky, where the stars are.

Haven't you seen how eager they are to get there? Don't you know why they are in such a hurry?

Of course, I can guess to whom they raise their arms: they have their mother as I have my own.

23. 商人

想象一下,妈妈,假设您待在家里,而我到外地旅行。

想象我的船已经载满了货物,准备启航。

现在,好好想想再告诉我,妈妈,我回来时应该带什么东西给您。

✺

妈妈,您想要成堆的黄金吗?

看呀,在金黄河流的两岸,田野里全都是金色谷物。

THE MERCHANT

Imagine, mother, that you are to stay at home and I am to travel into strange lands.

Imagine that my boat is ready at the landing fully laden.

Now think well, mother, before you say what I shall bring for you when I come back.

Mother, do you want heaps and heaps of gold?

There, by the banks of golden streams, fields are full of golden harvest.

而林荫下的林间小径,金色花落满地。

我会将之全部拾起,装在好几百只篮子里。

妈妈,您想要像秋天雨点般大的珍珠吗?

我会渡海到珍珠岛岸。在那里,珍珠在清晨曙光中,向草地上的花朵颤动着,珍珠落在草叶间,被狂野的浪涛喷洒在沙滩上。

哥哥呢,应该拥有一对长着翅膀、可以飞上云端的马。

而我应该带支魔术笔给父亲,他想都不用想,字便自己写了出来。

您呢,妈妈,我一定要拿到那只值上七个王国的珠宝箱送给您。

And in the shade of the forest path the golden champa flowers drop on the ground.

I will gather them all for you in many hundred baskets.

Mother, do you want pearls big as the raindrops of autumn?

I shall cross to the pearl island shore. There in the early morning light pearls tremble on the meadow flowers, pearls drop on the grass, and pearls are scattered on the sand in spray by the wild sea-waves.

My brother shall have a pair of horses with wings to fly among the clouds.

For father I shall bring a magic pen that, without his knowing, will write of itself.

For you, mother, I must have the casket and jewel that cost seven kings their kingdoms.

24. 同情

如果我只是只小小狗，不是您的孩子，亲爱的妈妈，当我想吃您碟子里的食物时，您会对我说"不"吗？

您会不会赶我走，对我说："走开，你这顽皮的小狗！"

那么我会走，妈妈，我会走的！您再怎么叫我，我都不会再到您身边，也绝不会再要您喂我了。

SYMPATHY

If I were only a little puppy, not your baby, mother dear, would you say "No" to me if I tried to eat from your dish?

Would you drive me off, saying to me, "Get away, you naughty little puppy?"

Then go, mother, go! I will never come to you when you call me, and never let you feed me any more.

如果我只是一只小小的绿色鹦鹉,不是您的宝贝,亲爱的妈妈,您会怕我飞走而用链子绑着我吗?

您会不会晃动手指对我说:"真是只不知感恩的可恶小鸟!每天每夜都啃咬着链子。"

那么我会走,妈妈,我会走的!我会跑到林子里,永远不会再让您将我抱在您的臂弯里。

If I were only a little green parrot, and not your baby, mother dear, would you keep me chained lest I should fly away?

Would you shake your finger at me and say, "What an ungrateful wretch of a bird! It is gnawing at its chain day and night?"

Then, go, mother, go! I will run away into the woods; I will never let you take me in your arms again.

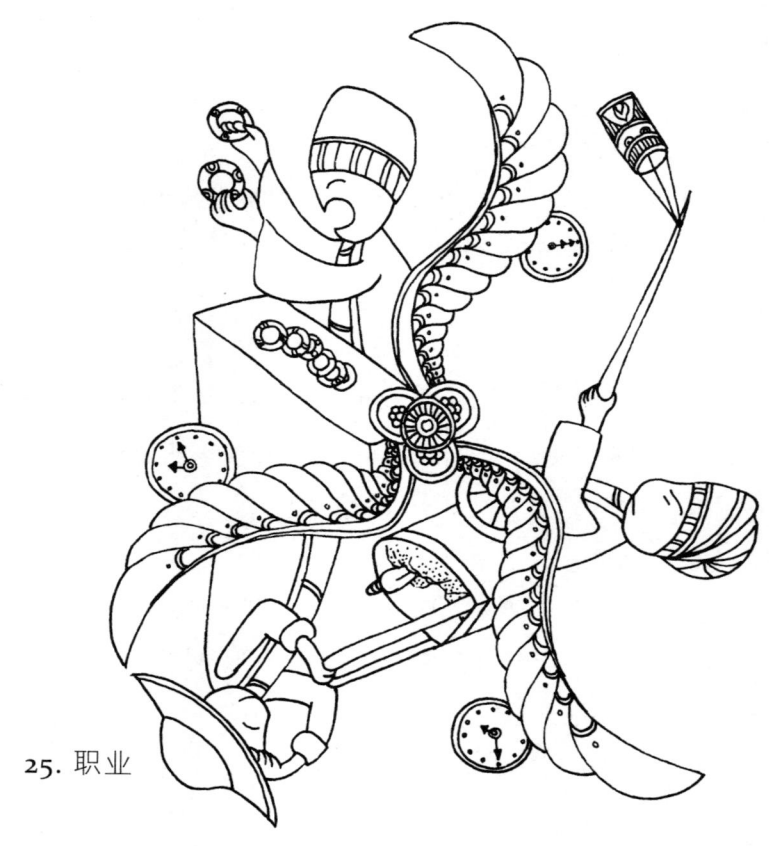

25. 职业

早晨钟敲十下时,我沿着我们的小巷走路上学去。

我每天都会遇到一名小贩喊着:"手镯,亮晶晶的手镯!"

他一点也不赶时间,没有固定要走的路线,没有他一定要去的地方,也不一定什么时间就得赶回到家。

我真希望自己是个小贩,整天在街上喊着:"手镯,亮晶晶的手镯!"

VOCATION

When the gong sounds ten in the morning and I walk to school by our lane,

Every day I meet the hawker crying, "Bangles, crystal bangles!"

There is nothing to hurry him on, there is no road he must take, no place he must go to, no time when he must come home.

I wish I were a hawker, spending my day in the road, crying, "Bangles, crystal bangles!"

下午四点,我从学校回来。

从一户人家的大门,我看到里面有位园丁在掘着地。

他拿着锄头,爱挖什么就挖什么,衣服都被泥土弄脏了。要是他让太阳晒黑了或被雨淋湿了,也没人会骂他。

我真希望自己是个园丁,爱怎么在园里挖地,都不会有人来阻止我。

晚上天一黑,妈妈就要我上床睡觉。

我从开着的窗口看到巡夜人来回走着。

那条路又暗又寂静,街灯就像头上长只红眼睛的巨人站在那里。

巡夜人晃着灯笼,影子随行在侧,他一生从未上床睡过一觉。

我真希望自己是个巡夜人,整晚在街上走着,提着灯笼追着影子跑。

When at four in the afternoon I come back from the school.

I can see through the gate of that house the gardener digging the ground.

He does what he likes with his spade, he soils his clothes with dust, nobody takes him to task if he gets baked in the sun or gets wet.

I wish I were a gardener digging away at the garden with nobody to stop me from digging.

Just as it gets dark in the evening and my mother sends me to bed.

I can see through my open window the watchman walking up and down.

The lane is dark and lonely, and the street-lamp stands like a giant with one red eye in its head.

The watchman swings his lantern and walks with his shadow at his side, and never once goes to bed in his life.

I wish I were a watchman walking the streets all night, chasing the shadows with my lantern.

26. 长者

妈妈,您的孩子真傻!她可真幼稚!

竟然分不清街灯与星星的差别。

当我们玩着拿石头当食物的游戏时,她还真以为那是可以吃的东西,想把石头放进嘴巴里。

当我在她面前翻开书,要她学a、b、c时,她竟然把书撕破,还莫名其妙地开心胡嚷;您的孩子就是这样读书的。

SUPERIOR

Mother, your baby is silly! She is so absurdly childish!

She does not know the difference between the lights in the streets and the stars.

When we play at eating with pebbles, she thinks they are real food, and tries to put them into her mouth.

When I open a book before her and ask her to learn her a, b, c, she tears the leaves with her hands and roars for joy at nothing; this is your baby's way of doing her lesson.

当我生气地对她摇摇头,责骂她,并说她顽皮时,她却哈哈大笑,觉得那很好玩。

大家都知道父亲不在,但是玩游戏时,假使我喊道:"爸爸",她仍会兴奋地四处张望,以为爸爸就在附近。

当我把我们洗衣工用来载衣服的驴子当学生,并且警告她说我是校长时,她依然莫名其妙地乱叫,喊我哥哥。

您的孩子想抓住月亮。她真好笑呢,还把甘尼许①喊成了甘奴许。

妈妈,您的孩子真傻,她可真幼稚!

---

① 甘尼许(Ganesh)是普遍常见的印度名字,同时也是象神之名。

When I shake my head at her in anger and scold her and call her naughty, she laughs and thinks it great fun.

Everybody knows that father is away, but if in play I call aloud "Father," she looks about her in excitement and thinks that father is near.

When I hold my class with the donkeys that our washerman brings to carry away the clothes and I warn her that I am the schoolmaster, she will scream for no reason and call me dada.

Your baby wants to catch the moon. She is so funny; she calls Ganesh Ganush.

Mother, your baby is silly, she is so absurdly childish!

27. 小大人

我个子小,因为我还是个小孩。等我到了像爸爸的年纪时,个儿就会变大了。

老师过来跟我说:"时候不早了,去把你的板子和书拿过来。"

我会告诉他:"您难道不知道我已经大得像爸爸,不再需要读书了吗?"

老师觉得奇怪地说:"他想的话,可以不用读书,因为他已经长大了。"

我自己穿好衣服,准备到拥挤的市集去。

叔叔赶过来说:"你会走丢的,我的孩子。让我带你去吧!"

THE LITTLE BIG MAN

I am small because I am a little child. I shall be big when I am as old as my father is.

My teacher will come and say, "It is late, bring your slate and your books."

I shall tell him, "Do you not know I am as big as father? And I must not have lessons any more."

My master will wonder and say, "He can leave his books if he likes, for he is grown up."

I shall dress myself and walk to the fair where the crowd is thick.

My uncle will come rushing up to me and say, "You will get lost, my boy; let me carry you."

我会回答:"难道您看不出来么,叔叔?我已经大得像爸爸了,我得自己走去市集。"

叔叔会说:"是的,他可以去任何他想去的地方,因为他已经长大了。"

I shall answer,"Can't you see, uncle, I am as big as father? I must go to the fair alone."

Uncle will say,"Yes, he can go wherever he likes, for he is grown up."

✿

　　妈妈沐浴回来时看到我拿钱给保姆,因为我已经知道怎么自己拿钥匙开钱盒了。

　　妈妈问说:"你在做什么,调皮的孩子?"

　　我会告诉她:"妈妈,难道您不知道,我已经大得像爸爸了,我得拿钱给保姆。"

　　妈妈会对自己说:"他可以拿钱给他想给的人,因为他已经长大了。"

　　爸爸十月放假回来时,以为我还是个孩子,而从城里带一些小鞋子、小绸衫回来给我。

　　我会说:"爸爸,把那些给哥哥吧,因为我已经长得跟您一样大了。"

　　父亲将想了一下后说:"他想要的话,可以自己去买衣服,因为他已经长大了。"

Mother will come from her bath when I am giving money to my nurse, for I shall know how to open the box with my key.

Mother will say, "What are you about, naughty child?"

I shall tell her, "Mother, don't you know, I am as big as father, and I must give silver to my nurse."

Mother will say to herself, "He can give money to whom he likes, for he is grown up."

In the holiday time in October father will come home and, thinking that I am still a baby, will bring for me from the town little shoes and small silken frocks.

I shall say, "Father, give them to my dada, for I am as big as you are."

Father will think and say, "He can buy his own clothes if he likes, for he is grown up."

28. 十二点钟

妈妈,我现在真的不想做功课,我已经读了一整个早上的书了。

您说现在才十二点钟。即使现在还不到十二点钟,您就不能把十二点想成是下午了吗?

我轻而易举便可将这时的太阳想成已经落到稻田边啦,老渔妇在池塘边采着晚餐要吃的野菜。

我只要一闭上眼,便能想象得到马达树①下的影子越来越深暗,池里的水黑得发亮。

要是十二点钟能在午夜里降临,那么黑夜为何不能在正午十二点钟报到呢?

---

① 孟加拉国语为马达树(Madar),即中文的"牛角瓜",别称"皇冠花",属于直立灌木植物。

TWELVE O' CLOCK

Mother, I do want to leave off my lessons now. I have been at my book all the morning.

You say it is only twelve o'clock. Suppose it isn't any later; can't you ever think it is afternoon when it is only twelve o'clock?

I can easily imagine now that the sun has reached the edge of that rice-field, and the old fisher-woman is gathering herbs for her supper by the side of the pond.

I can just shut my eyes and think that the shadows are growing darker under the madar tree, and the water in the pond looks shiny black.

If twelve o'clock can come in the night, why can't the night come when it is twelve o'clock?

29. 作者

您说爸爸写了很多书,但我看不懂他写的东西。

他整个晚上都在读给您听,可是您真的了解他写的东西吗?

妈妈,您跟我们讲的故事多有趣呀!我想不懂,为什么爸爸就不能写那样的故事呢?

难道他从没听他妈妈讲过巨人、精灵和公主的故事吗?

莫非他全都忘记了?

他常很晚才沐浴,还得让您去叫他上百次。

您候着并帮他热好食物,但他还是继续埋头写作,忘了所有的事情。

父亲总是在玩写书的游戏。

AUTHORSHIP

You say that father writes a lot of books, but what he writes I don't understand.

He was reading to you all the evening, but could you really make out what he meant?

What nice stories, mother, you can tell us! Why can't father write like that, I wonder?

Did he never hear from his own mother stories of giants and fairies and princesses?

Has he forgotten them all?

Often when he gets late for his bath you have to go and call him an hundred times.

You wait and keep his dishes warm for him, but he goes on writing and forgets.

Father always plays at making books.

要是我到爸爸的房里玩,您会过来念我:"真是顽皮的孩子!"

要是我发出一丁点声响,您便会说:"你没看到父亲正在工作吗?"

老是在写作到底有什么好玩的呀?

当我拿起父亲的钢笔或铅笔,学他在他的书上写:a、b、c、d、e、f、g、h、i时,您为什么会对我发脾气呢,妈妈?

爸爸写的时候,您可从未说过一句。

爸爸浪费那么多纸张,妈妈,您似乎一点也不在意。

但只要我拿一张纸做船时,您就会说:"孩子,你真讨厌!"

爸爸在一张又一张的纸两面都涂满了黑色记号,您又是怎么想的呢?

If ever I go to play in father's room, you come and call me, "What a naughty child! "

If I make the slightest noise, you say, "Don't you see that father's at his work? "

What's the fun of always writing and writing?

When I take up father's pen or pencil and write upon his book just as he does,—a, b, c, d, e, f, g, h, i,—why do you get cross with me, then, mother?

You never say a word when father writes.

When my father wastes such heaps of paper, mother, you don't seem to mind at all.

But if I take only one sheet to make a boat with, you say, "Child, how troublesome you are! "

What do you think of father's spoiling sheets and sheets of paper with black marks all over on both sides?

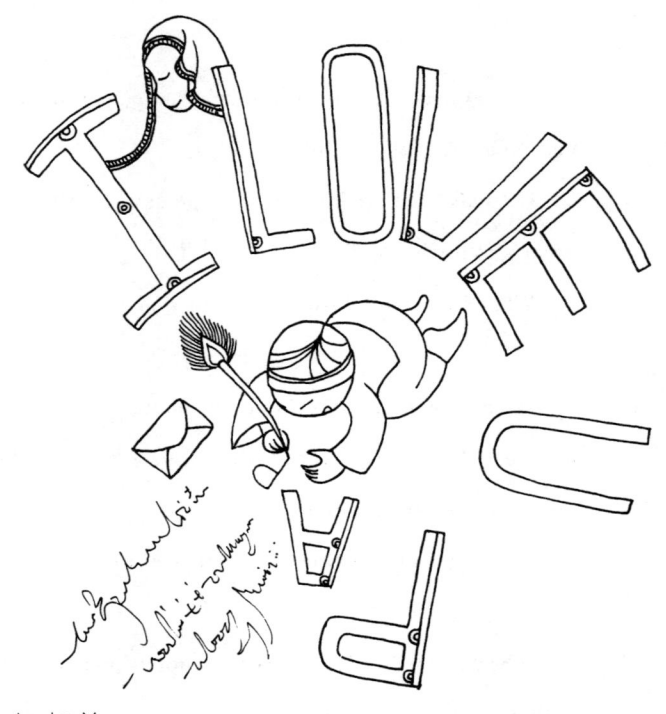

30. 坏邮差

亲爱的妈妈,跟我说说,您为什么如此安静沉默地坐在地上?

雨从开着的窗子打进来,您都淋湿了,却似乎不在意。

您听到钟声敲四下了吗?该是哥哥放学回家的时候了。

到底发生了什么事?您的神色看起来好奇怪。

您今天没收到爸爸的信吗?

THE WICKED POSTMAN

Why do you sit there on the floor so quiet and silent, tell me, mother dear?

The rain is coming in through the open window, making you all wet, and you don't mind it.

Do you hear the gong striking four? It is time for my brother to come home from school.

What has happened to you that you look so strange?

Haven't you got a letter from father to-day?

我看见邮差的袋里装满了信,几乎镇上每个人都收到信了。

只有爸爸的信,被他留下来自己看了。我可以确定那邮差是个坏人。

但别因此而伤心呀,亲爱的妈妈。

明天是隔壁村落的市集日,您可以请女佣去帮您买些笔和纸。

所有爸爸该写的信都由我来写,您不会找到半点儿破绽。

我会从 A 一直写到 K。

但是,妈妈,您为什么笑了呢?

您不相信我能写得跟爸爸一样好吗?

我会用心写整齐,把每个字母写得又大又漂亮。

我写完之后,您以为我会跟爸爸一样傻,将信放进那可恶邮差的袋里吗?

我会自己马上将这些信送来给您,并且逐字逐句帮您读。

我知道那个邮差不愿意把真正很棒的信件送来给您。

I saw the postman bringing letters in his bag for almost everybody in the town.

Only, father's letters he keeps to read himself. I am sure the postman is a wicked man.

But don't be unhappy about that, mother dear.

To-morrow is market day in the next village. You ask your maid to buy some pens and papers.

I myself will write all father's letters; you will not find a single mistake.

I shall write from A right up to K.

But, mother, why do you smile?

You don't believe that I can write as nicely as father does!

But I shall rule my paper carefully, and write all the letters beautifully big.

When I finish my writing, do you think I shall be so foolish as father and drop it into the horrid postman's bag?

I shall bring it to you myself without waiting, and letter by letter help you to read my writing.

I know the postman does not like to give you the really nice letters.

31. 英雄

妈妈,让我们想象彼此身在旅途上,正通过一个危险的陌生国度。

您坐在一顶轿子里,而我骑着一匹红色骏马跑在您身边。

那已是晚上,太阳下山了。约拉狄西荒地黯淡无光地在我们面前展开。大地贫瘠又荒芜。

您吓坏了,在心里想道:"我真不晓得我们到了什么地方啦。"

我跟您说:"妈妈,您别害怕。"

THE HERO

Mother, let us imagine we are travelling, and passing through a strange and dangerous country.

You are riding in a palanquin and I am trotting by you on a red horse.

It is evening and the sun goes down. The waste of Joradighi lies wan and grey before us. The land is desolate and barren.

You are frightened and thinking—"I know not where we have come to."

I say to you,"Mother, do not be afraid."

草地上长满带刺的草,有条崎岖小径穿越其间。

在这片浩瀚原野上,看不见任何牛群。它们全回到村里的牛棚了。

天色暗了下来,大地和天空都显得朦胧昏暗,我们也分不清自己正往哪里走。

您突然叫了我一声,低语问道:"河岸边那是什么火光呀?"

就在那时,一阵可怕的叫声突然从那里发出,幢幢人影朝我们跑来。

您蹲坐在轿子里,喃喃祷念着众神的名字。

轿夫们则吓得直发抖,躲进荆棘丛里去了。

我向您喊道:"别害怕,妈妈,有我在这里。"

The meadow is prickly with spiky grass, and through it runs a narrow broken path.

There are no cattle to be seen in the wide field; they have gone to their village stalls.

It grows dark and dim on the land and sky, and we cannot tell where we are going.

Suddenly you call me and ask me in a whisper, "What light is that near the bank? "

Just then there bursts out a fearful yell, and figures come running towards us.

You sit crouched in your palanquin and repeat the names of the gods in prayer.

The bearers, shaking in terror, hide themselves in the thorny bush.

I shout to you, "Don't be afraid, mother, I am here. "

他们手持着长木棍，满头散发，越跑越近。

我喊道："小心啦！你们这些坏蛋！再往前走一步，你们就没命了。"

他们又发出一阵可怕的叫声，往前冲了过来。

您抓住我的手，说道："亲爱的孩子，看在上帝的份儿上，躲开他们吧。"

我回道："妈妈，您在旁边看着就好。"

接着我策马飞奔，剑与盾铿锵互相撞击着。

战斗变得如此激烈，妈妈，要是您从轿子里看得见，肯定吓得直打冷战。

他们之中许多人逃走了，也有很多人被砍成碎片。

我知道您自己一个人坐在那里时，准在心里想着，您的孩子这次肯定逃不过了。

但我全身溅满血，跑到您身边说："妈妈，战斗结束了。"

您走出轿子亲吻着我，把我抱在您怀中，

自言自语地说："要是没有我的孩子保护我，我可真不知道该如何是好了。"

With long sticks in their hands and hair all wild about their heads, they come nearer and nearer.

I shout,"Have a care! You villains! One step more and you are dead men. "

They give another terrible yell and rush forward.

You clutch my hand and say,"Dear boy, for heaven's sake, keep away from them. "

I say,"Mother, just you watch me. "

Then I spur my horse for a wild gallop, and my sword and buckler clash against each other.

The fight becomes so fearful, mother, that it would give you a cold shudder could you see it from your palanquin.

Many of them fly, and a great number are cut to pieces.

I know you are thinking, sitting all by yourself, that your boy must be dead by this time.

But I come to you all stained with blood, and say,"Mother, the fight is over now. "

You come out and kiss me, pressing me to your heart,

and you say to yourself,"I don't know what I should do if I hadn't my boy to escort me. "

上千件无聊的事情日复一日发生，为什么这种事不能够偶尔出现呢？

就像书中的故事。

哥哥会说："那有可能吗？我老觉得他弱不禁风的。"

我们村里的乡亲全要惊讶地说："还好有那孩子跟他妈妈在一起，真是万幸，可不是吗？"

A thousand useless things happen day after day, and why couldn't such a thing come true by chance?

It would be like a story in a book.

My brother would say, "Is it possible? I always thought he was so delicate!"

Our village people would all say in amazement, "Was it not lucky that the boy was with his mother?"

32. 告别

该是我离开的时候了,妈妈,我得走了。

在清寂晨幕的灰暗天色里,您伸了伸手想抱抱床上的宝贝,我得跟您说:"宝贝不在那儿了!"——妈妈,我得走了。

我会化作一缕轻风,照拂着您;当您沐浴时,我会变成水中的涟漪,一次又一次亲吻您。

在风雨不宁的夜晚,当雨滴拍打叶片时,您躺在床上会听见我的呢喃,我的笑声也会随着闪电之光从敞开的窗子照进您房里。

如果您躺在那儿思念您的孩子,直到半夜还睡不着,我会从星空中哼歌给您听:"睡吧,妈妈,睡吧。"

我会趁您睡着时,随着游移月光偷偷爬上您的床,躺在您怀里。

THE END

It is time for me to go, mother; I am going.

When in the paling darkness of the lonely dawn you stretch out your arms for your baby in the bed, I shall say, "Baby is not there!"—mother, I am going.

I shall become a delicate draught of air and caress you; and I shall be ripples in the water when you bathe, and kiss you and kiss you again.

In the gusty night when the rain patters on the leaves you will hear my whisper in your bed, and my laughter will flash with the lightning through the open window into your room.

If you lie awake, thinking of your baby till late into the night, I shall sing to you from the stars, "Sleep mother, sleep."

On the straying moonbeams I shall steal over your bed, and lie upon your bosom while you sleep.

我会变成梦,从您微张的眼帘偷溜进您的深眠中;当您醒来,惊讶地看着四周时,我便像闪烁的萤火消失在黑暗中。

而在普耶节①这热闹节庆,邻居孩子们来家里四处跑跳玩闹着时,我会融入笛子的乐音里,整日回荡在您心中。

亲爱的阿姨将带着普耶礼物来,问道:"你的孩子呢,妹妹?"妈妈,您会温柔地告诉她:"他在我的眼睛里,在我的身体里,也在我的灵魂里。"

---

① 普耶节,即是印度十月间的"难近母祭日"。难近母为古婆罗门教中最早崇拜的女神之一,常见形象为三眼十手,骑着狮或虎。

I shall become a dream, and through the little opening of your eyelids I shall slip into the depths of your sleep; and when you wake up and look round startled, like a twinkling firefly I shall flit out into the darkness.

When, on the great festival of puja, the neighbours' children come and play about the house, I shall melt into the music of the flute and throb in your heart all day.

Dear auntie will come with puja-presents and will ask, "Where is our baby, sister?" Mother, you will tell her softly, "He is in the pupils of my eyes, he is in my body and in my soul."

33. 呼唤

她离去时夜空已经全黑,他们都睡着了。

现在天色依然乌暗,我四处喊着她:"回来吧,亲爱的!大地还在沉睡,当星星互相凝视时,你偷偷来一会儿,没人会发现的。"

她在树梢刚萌芽、春天初抵时离去。

现在花朵已经盛开了,我喊着:"回来吧,亲爱的!孩子们在漫不经心的游戏中,将花捡拾在一起,又把花抛撒开。要是你来拿走一朵小花,没人会知道少了一朵的。"

THE RECALL

The night was dark when she went away, and they slept.

The night is dark now, and I call for her, "Come back, my darling; the world is asleep; and no one would know, if you came for a moment while stars are gazing at stars. "

She went away when the trees were in bud and the spring was young.

Now the flowers are in high bloom and I call, "Come back, my darling. The children gather and scatter flowers in reckless sport. And if you come and take one little blossom no one will miss it. "

那些只知道玩耍的人,还是一直在玩,如此地虚掷生命。

我听着那些谈话,并喊道:"回来吧,我亲爱的!妈妈心中充满了爱,你来接受她一个小小的吻,没有人会嫉妒的。"

Those that used to play are playing still, so spendthrift is life.

I listen to their chatter and call, "Come back, my darling, for mother's heart is full to the brim with love, and if you come to snatch only one little kiss from her no one will grudge it."

34. 最初的茉莉

啊，这些茉莉花，这些白色的茉莉花！

我似犹记得自己第一次满手捧着这些茉莉花的模样，这些白色的茉莉花。

我爱着阳光、天空及绿色大地；

我在午夜的黑暗中，听到潺潺流水声；

秋天落日在荒寂的弯路上洒落我身，就像一名掀起头纱接受爱人的新娘。

THE FIRST JASMINES

Ah, these jasmines, these white jasmines!

I seem to remember the first day when I filled my hands with these jasmines, these white jasmines.

I have loved the sunlight, the sky and the green earth;

I have heard the liquid murmur of the river through the darkness of midnight;

Autumn sunsets have come to me at the bend of a road in the lonely waste, like a bride raising her veil to accept her lover.

然而我仍甜蜜地记得小时候第一次满手捧着白色茉莉花的模样。

　　我生命中曾有过许多快活时光，曾在节庆夜晚随着制造欢笑的人笑过。

　　在烟雨蒙蒙的清晨，我吟唱过许多浪漫诗歌。

　　我宴会晚装的脖颈上也曾戴过爱人的手编花环。

　　然而我仍甜蜜地记得小时候第一次满手捧着白色茉莉花的模样。

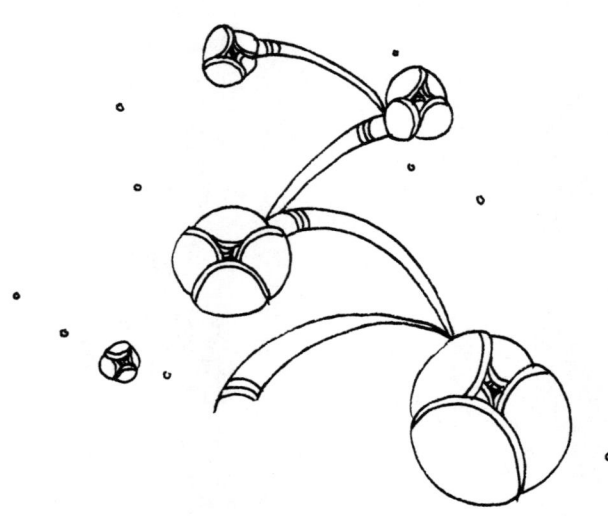

Yet my memory is still sweet with the first white jasmines that I held in my hand when I was a child.

Many a glad day has come in my life, and I have laughed with merrymakers on festival nights.

On grey mornings of rain I have crooned many an idle song.

I have worn round my neck the evening wreath of bakulas woven by the hand of love.

Yet my heart is sweet with the memory of the first fresh jasmines that filled my hands when I was a child.

35. 榕树

喔！你这棵顶着满头乱发站在池边的榕树，是否已经忘了那个跟鸟儿一样在你枝头上筑巢又离开了你的小孩？

难道你不记得他是怎么坐在窗边，想着你纠缠的根到底是怎样扎进地下的？

THE BANYAN TREE

O you shaggy-headed banyan tree standing on the bank of the pond, have you forgotten the little child, like the birds that have nested in your branches and left you?

Do you not remember how he sat at the window and wondered at the tangle of your roots that plunged underground?

妇人会带着她们的水罐到池边装水，而你大大的黑影在水中晃动着，就像在睡梦中挣扎着要起来似的。

阳光在水波上漫舞，好似不眠不休的梭机，织着金黄色的毯子。

两只鸭子于芦苇边倒影上游着，而那个小孩仍静静地坐在那里思考。

他渴望成为风，吹过你摇曳的树枝；想成为你的影子，随着日光增长；想成为鸟儿，栖息在你最顶端的树枝上；还想像那两只鸭子在芦苇与倒影间穿梭。

The women would come to fill their jars in the pond, and your huge black shadow would wriggle on the water like sleep struggling to wake up.

Sunlight danced on the ripples like restless tiny shuttles weaving golden tapestry.

Two ducks swam by the weedy margin above their shadows, and the child would sit still and think.

He longed to be the wind and blow through your rustling branches, to be your shadow and lengthen with the day on the water, to be a bird and perch on your top-most twig, and to float like those ducks among the weeds and shadows.

36. 祝福

祝福这小小的心灵，这洁白的灵魂，已经为我们的大地赢得了天堂之吻。

他喜爱阳光，喜爱见到妈妈的脸庞。

他并没有学到厌恶尘土、渴求黄金。

将他紧紧拥在怀里，好好祝福他。

他来到这满是歧路的土地。

我不知道他是如何从人群中选中你，进而来到你家门口，抓着你的手请求指引的。

他跟随你，笑笑又说说，心底不存半点怀疑。

莫辜负他的信任，带领他走向正道，好好祝福他。

将你的手贴放在他头上祈祷，即使波涛底下渐趋险峻，风仍有可能从天而降，鼓起他的船帆，将他推往平和的避风港。

别在忙碌中将他遗忘，让他来到你心房，好好祝福他。

BENEDICTION

Bless this little heart, this white soul that has won the kiss of heaven for our earth.

He loves the light of the sun, he loves the sight of his mother's face.

He has not learned to despise the dust, and to hanker after gold.

Clasp him to your heart and bless him.

He has come into this land of an hundred cross-roads.

I know not how he chose you from the crowd came to your door, and grasped your hand to ask his way.

He will follow you, laughing and talking, and not a doubt in his heart.

Keep his trust, lead him straight and bless him.

Lay your hand on his head, and pray that though the waves underneath grow threatening, yet the breath from above may come and fill his sails and waft him to the haven of peace.

Forget him not in your hurry, let him come to your heart and bless him.

37. 礼物

我想给你点东西,我的孩子,因我们都漂流在世界之河中。

我们的生命将分道扬镳,爱也会被遗忘。

但我并没有傻到希冀拿礼物来收买你的心。

你的生命正青春,路还长着,你一口气饮尽我们给你的爱,接着便转身从我们身边跑开了。

你有自己的玩乐及玩伴,没时间或没心思想到我们,这又有什么伤害呢?

而我们呢,年老时确实有的是时间去细数过往的日子,将从我们手中永远失去的事物珍藏在心里。

河流唱着歌匆匆流去,冲破所有屏障。但是青山犹在,记念着种种,并以其不朽之爱相随。

THE GIFT

I want to give you something, my child, for we are drifting in the stream of the world.

Our lives will be carried apart, and our love forgotten.

But I am not so foolish as to hope that I could buy your heart with my gifts.

Young is your life, your path long, and you drink the love we bring you at one draught and turn and run away from us.

You have your play and your playmates. What harm is there if you have no time or thought for us.

We, indeed, have leisure enough in old age to count the days that are past, to cherish in our hearts what our hands have lost for ever.

The river runs swift with a song, breaking through all barriers. But the mountain stays and remembers, and follows her with his love.

38. 我的歌

  我的这首歌会扬起乐音环绕着你,我的孩子,好似爱的柔情臂弯。

  我的这首歌将吻触你的额头,宛如祝福之吻。

  当你独处时,它会陪伴在你身边,于你耳畔微语;当你在拥挤的人群时,它会让你超然世外,守护着你。

MY SONG

This song of mine will wind its music around you, my child, like the fond arms of love.

This song of mine will touch your forehead like a kiss of blessing.

When you are alone it will sit by your side and whisper in your ear, when you are in the crowd it will fence you about with aloofness.

我的歌将化为你梦中的双翼,将你的心带往未知的岸边。

当黑夜覆没你的道路时,它会像一颗忠心的星辰照在你前头。

我的歌会驻进你的瞳孔里,将你的视线带往事物的中心。

当我的声音因死亡而静寂时,我的歌会在你鲜活的心中唱说着。

My song will be like a pair of wings to your dreams, it will transport your heart to the verge of the unknown.

It will be like the faithful star overhead when dark night is over your road.

My song will sit in the pupils of your eyes, and will carry your sight into the heart of things.

And when my voice is silent in death, my song will speak in your living heart.

39. 孩子天使

他们喧闹争吵着,他们失望猜疑,知道他们的争辩永远也没个终了。

让你的生命进到他们之间去,我的孩子,宛若安定又纯洁的光明之火,让他们欢乐得沉静下来。

他们在贪婪与嫉妒中是残暴的,他们的话语宛如隐藏的刀刃,渴欲饮血。

THE CHILD-ANGEL

They clamour and fight, they doubt and despair, they know no end to their wranglings.

Let your life come amongst them like a flame of light, my child, unflickering and pure, and delight them into silence.

They are cruel in their greed and their envy, their words are like hidden knives thirsting for blood.

去站在他们愤恨不平的心中，我的孩子，以你温柔的眼眸看向他们，犹如夜晚宽容的和平，盖过白日的纷扰。

让他们看看你的脸，我的孩子，让他们因此了解所有事物的真义；让他们爱你，进而使他们彼此互爱。

来到无垠的怀抱中坐下吧，我的孩子。当旭日初升，让你的心亦如盛开的花朵般打开来，待日落时低下你的头，在沉默中完成这一天的祷告。

Go and stand amidst their scowling hearts, my child, and let your gentle eyes fall upon them like the forgiving peace of the evening over the strife of the day.

Let them see your face, my child, and thus know the meaning of all things; let them love you and thus love each other.

Come and take your seat in the bosom of the limitless, my child. At sunrise open and raise your heart like a blossoming flower, and at sunset bend your head and in silence complete the worship of the day.

40. 最后的买卖

"来雇用我吧!"当我早晨在铺石路上走着时,我这么喊道。

国王驾着他的战车,手持着剑走来。

他拉起我的手说:"我以我的权力雇用你。"

但是他的权力毫无用处,他登上他的战车离开了。

日正当中时,家家户户都紧闭门户。

我独自在某条蜿蜒小巷走着。

有位老人拿着一袋金子走出来。

他想了一下,说道:"我用我的钱雇用你。"

他逐一数着他的金币,我却转身离开。

THE LAST BARGAIN

"Come and hire me, "I cried, while in the morning I was walking on the stone-paved road.

Sword in hand, the King came in his chariot.

He held my hand and said,"I will hire you with my power."

But his power counted for nought, and he went away in his chariot.

In the heat of the midday the houses stood with shut doors.

I wandered along the crooked lane.

An old man came out with his bag of gold.

He pondered and said,"I will hire you with my money."

He weighed his coins one by one, but I turned away.

将近黄昏,园子的篱笆开满了花。

一名美女走出来,对我说:"我以我的微笑雇用你。"

她的微笑黯淡下来化成了泪珠,又独自走回黑暗中。

太阳在沙地上闪耀着,海浪恣意溅洒开来。

有个孩子坐在那里玩着贝壳。

他抬起头来,似乎认识我,开口说:"我两手空空雇用你。"

从那时起,在这孩童游戏中做成的买卖,令我成了自由人。

It was evening. The garden hedge was all aflower.

The fair maid came out and said, "I will hire you with a smile."

Her smile paled and melted into tears, and she went back alone into the dark.

The sun glistened on the sand, and the sea waves broke waywardly.

A child sat playing with shells.

He raised his head and seemed to know me, and said, "I hire you with nothing."

From thenceforward that bargain struck in child's play made me a free man.